THE ❄ TRUTH ❄ ABOUT

Hi THERE!

# SNOW PEOPLE

# THE ❄ TRUTH ❄ ABOUT
# SNOW
# PEOPLE

Compiled by Blue Lantern Studio

MMV 🐯 GREEN TIGER PRESS

There are snow people every place in the
world where snow falls.

They begin with a big snowball,
and then more snow is added until they come alive.

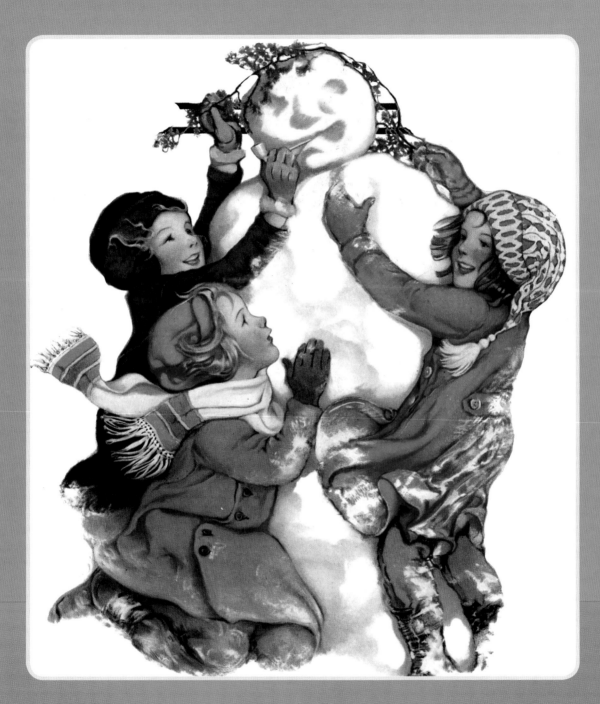

They need mouths and eyes and noses,
and many of them
have buttons, hats, and other useful things.

There are as many different personalities among
snow people as there are among humans.

There are also many
kinds of snow creatures.

Snow people love company of all kinds.

Snow people are always cheerful,

and are happiest when others are happy.

They make excellent friends.

They move around
more than most people realize,

...and like to be helpful whenever possible.

Snow people have many
interests, and sometimes take jobs.

All of them love games and play,

and are very good sports.

Christmas is their favorite time,
and they like to share their joy with others.

When it grows warm,

there comes the time of melting,

which seems sad.

However, then they go to live in Snowland,

and enjoy lives quite like our own,
waiting for winter to come
so they can join us again.

# SNOW PEOPLE PICTURE CREDITS